My New Friend Is So Fun!

To Nick Meglin, Tom Gammill, and all sorts of new friends

ISBN 978-1-338-34354-0

12 11 10 9 8 7 6 5 4 3 2 1   18 19 20 21 22 23

Printed in the U.S.A.   40

First Scholastic printing, September 2018

This book is set in Century/Monotype; Grilled Cheese BTN/Fontbros; Neutraface, Fink, Typography of Coop/House Industries; Billy/Fontspring.

An ELEPHANT & PIGGIE Book

SCHOLASTIC INC.

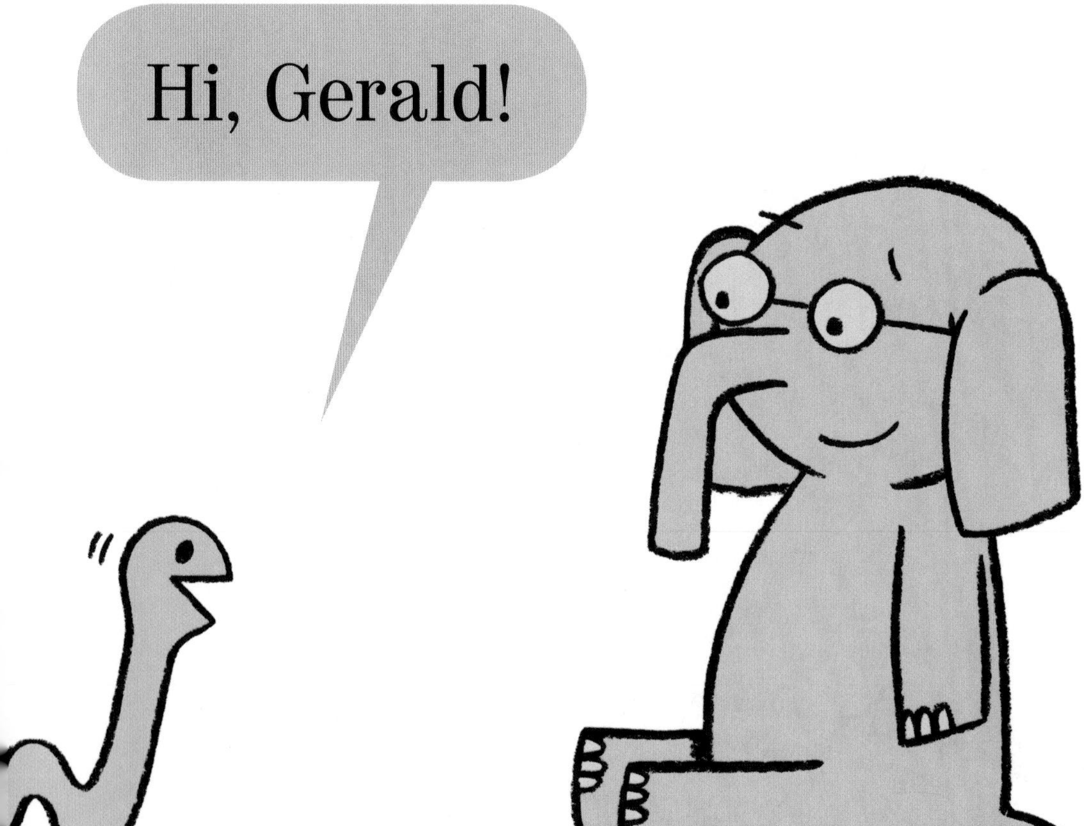
Hi, Gerald!

3

Piggie just met
Brian Bat for
the first time.

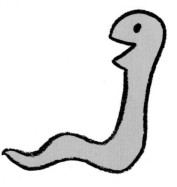

Now they
are playing.

Fun!

Brian Bat is nice!

7

Piggie is *my* Best Friend!

9

They must be having a *really* fun time!

Yeah!

They must be having
a *super* fun time!

Yeah!

12

13

15

17

19

24

25

SKID!

SKID!

35

We have
been playing
BEST
FRIEND
GAMES!

We even made
Best Friend
drawings!

Best. Friend.
Drawings?

45

Do you want
to see our
drawings?

47

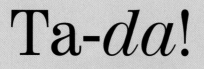

Ta-*da*!

49

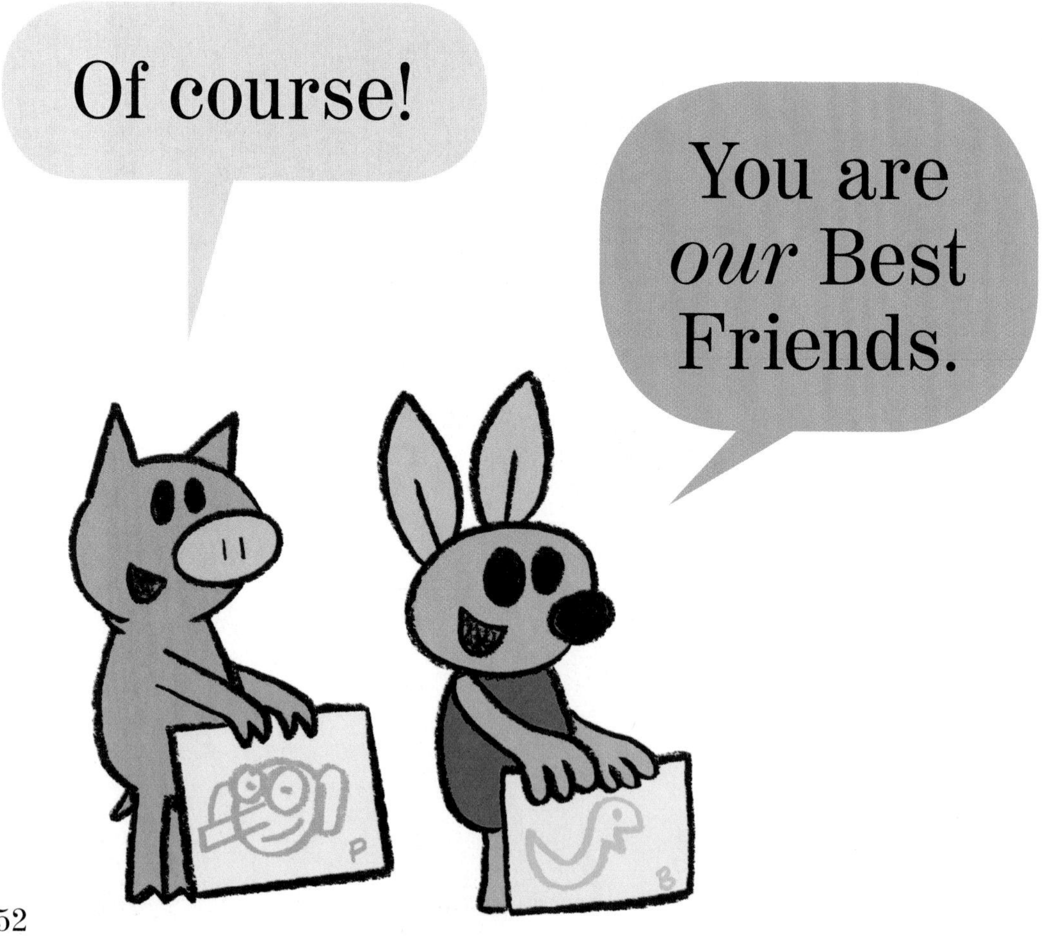
Of course!
You are *our* Best Friends.
P
B

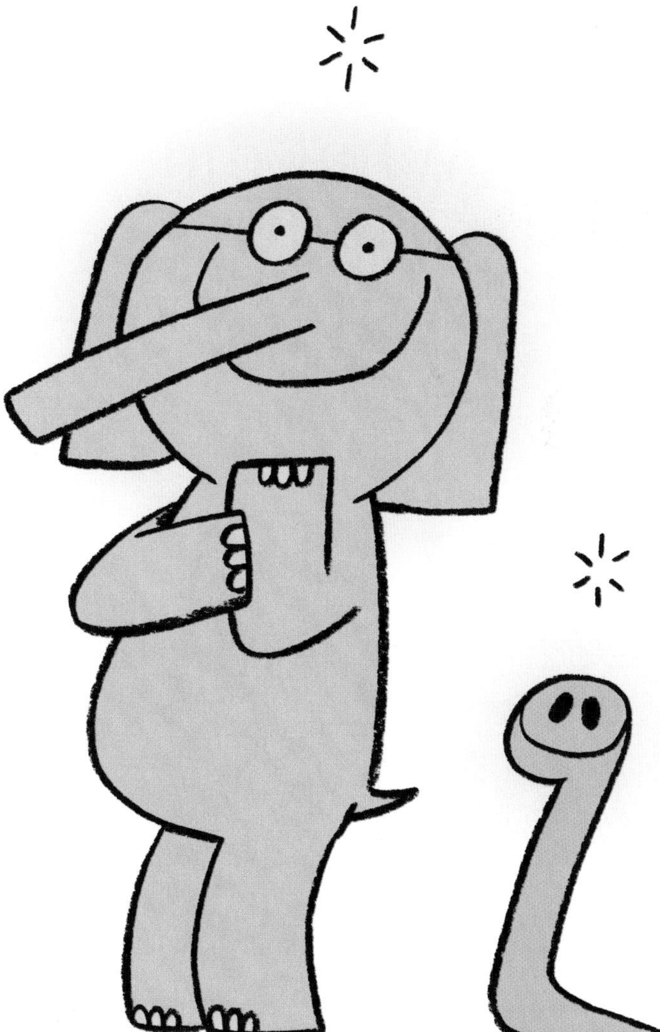

54

Have you read all of Elephant and Piggie's funny adventures?